618.1 GRE

Gregson, Susan R.
Premenstrual syndrome.

618.1 GRE

Gregson, Susan R.
Premenstrual syndrome.

Date Due	Borrower's Name	

Premenstrual Syndrome

Perspectives on Physical Health

by Susan R. Gregson

NIPHER LIBRARY

Consultant:
June LaValleur, MD, FACOG
Assistant Professor
Department of Obstetrics, Gynecology,
and Women's Health
University of Minnesota

LifeMatters
an imprint of Capstone Press
Mankato, Minnesota

LifeMatters Books are published by Capstone Press
PO Box 669 • 151 Good Counsel Drive • Mankato, Minnesota 56002
http://www.capstone-press.com

Printed in the United States of America

Library of Congress Cataloging-in-Publication Data
Gregson, Susan R.
      Premenstrual syndrome / by Susan R. Gregson.
            p.   cm.—(Perspectives on physical health)
      Includes bibliographical references and index.
      Summary: Discusses premenstrual syndrome, or PMS, its symptoms, and treatments.
      ISBN 0-7368-0421-8 (book)—ISBN 0-7368-0438-2 (series)
      1. Premenstrual syndrome—Juvenile literature. 2. Menstruation disorders—Juvenile literature. [1. Premenstrual syndrome. 2. Menstruation.] I. Title. II. Series.
      RG165 .G74 2000
      618.1´72—dc21   99-055030
                                                            CIP

Staff Credits
Rebecca Aldridge, editor; Adam Lazar, designer; Jodi Theisen, photo researcher

Photo Credits
Cover: PNI/©StockByte
FPG International/©VCG, 7; ©G. Randall, 16; ©Tony Anderson, 35
Index Stock Photography/8, 11, 37, 38, 42, 51
International Stock/©Sunstar, 32; ©Patrick Ramsey, 55, 56; ©Gerard Fritz, 59
PNI/©Digital Vision, 49
Unicorn Stock/©Jeff Greenberg, 19
Uniphoto/24; ©Llewellyn, 14, 45
Visuals Unlimited/©SIU, 29

A 0 9 8 7 6 5 4 3 2 1

Table of Contents

1	PMS and Menstruation	4
2	What Is PMS?	12
3	Tracking PMS	20
4	Making Healthy Changes	30
5	Diagnosing PMS	40
6	Treating PMS Symptoms	46
7	Taking Control of PMS	52
	Glossary	60
	For More Information	61
	Useful Addresses and Internet Sites	62
	Index	63

Chapter
Overview

Probably half of all females have symptoms of PMS just before they begin menstruation.

PMS is a common problem that can interfere with daily life.

PMS consists of more than 150 different physical and psychological symptoms.

Menstruation is just one part of a female's monthlong menstrual cycle.

PMS and Menstruation

Allena tried to pay attention to Mr. Ryan, who was at the front of

ALLENA, AGE 15

the classroom. Casey and Hope were whispering and giggling at their desks just behind Allena. Casey poked Allena in the side with a folded piece of paper. Allena took the paper from her. She unfolded the note and read it. It said, "Signs that you have PMS: Everyone around you has an attitude problem. Your favorite breakfast is a chocolate chip omelet. The dryer has shrunk every pair of your jeans. You're sure everyone is plotting to get you, even your baby sister. And your boyfriend suddenly agrees with everything you say."

No Laughing Matter

You probably have heard the jokes about premenstrual syndrome, or PMS. The jokes usually involve moody, angry girls or women who crave chocolate and drive their friends and family nuts. Different studies make varying estimates of how many women who menstruate, or have their period, have PMS. It is safe to say, however, that almost half of women who menstruate have symptoms of PMS.

PMS is a common problem that can interfere with daily life. It can affect how a woman feels physically and psychologically, or mentally. It can affect how she reacts to events happening in her life. Sometimes PMS strains her relationships with family and friends.

Many people still do not take PMS seriously or recognize it as a medical problem. The good news is that since the 1980s, PMS has been diagnosed, or recognized, as a real medical condition. Before that time, even doctors often would tell women that PMS was all in their head. Sometimes friends and family of people with PMS thought these women were lazy, weak, or just plain crazy.

Signs and Symptoms

PMS is a condition that a girl or woman can have a few days or two weeks before menstruation. It consists of more than 150 possible symptoms. A symptom is evidence of a medical condition. Some PMS symptoms are physical such as bloating, breast tenderness, or headaches. Other symptoms affect a person psychologically. Some of these symptoms may include moodiness or feelings of anxiety or anger. Things that normally would not bother a woman or girl may be irritating while she has PMS. People with PMS may have just one or two symptoms or they may have many. The symptoms might even change a little from month to month. Some of the most common PMS symptoms are listed on the next page.

Common Symptoms of PMS

Physical changes:

Acne, Rashes

Backaches

Bloating, Weight gain

Breast tenderness

Constipation (trouble getting rid of solid bodily waste) or

Diarrhea (a condition in which normally solid waste is runny and frequent)

Cravings, Appetite changes

Extreme tiredness

Joint pain

Light-headedness, Fainting

Nausea (feeling like you are going to throw up)

Vomiting (throwing up)

Psychological changes:

Anger

Anxiety

Confusion

Crying spells

Depression

Emotional upset

Forgetfulness, Memory loss

Irritability

Poor concentration

Tension

Unpredictable mood swings

In the United States, the average age when a girl first gets her period is 12. It is normal, however, to start as early as age 10 or as late as age 17.

DID YOU KNOW?

Puberty and Periods

A discussion about the female body and menstruation may make PMS easier to understand. Then you can better understand how it affects you, your mom, your sister, or your friends.

Girls begin their menstrual cycle during puberty. In girls, puberty usually happens between ages 9 and 17. During puberty, a girl's body physically changes as she becomes a woman. Her breasts develop and her hips get wider, among other changes. During puberty, the brain sends messages to the body telling it to produce sex hormones. These hormones are chemicals in the blood that control sexual development and body functions.

One female sex hormone is estrogen. This hormone tells the eggs in the ovaries, or female sex organs, to grow. The eggs have been in a female's ovaries even before birth. A one-month-old female fetus, or developing human, has eggs in the ovaries. Once puberty begins in a girl, the ovaries release one mature egg each month. This is called ovulation. The egg travels through a passageway called the fallopian tube. This tube leads to the uterus, which is a hollow, muscular organ lined with glands. This glandular lining is called the endometrium. The uterus is where an unborn baby grows and develops.

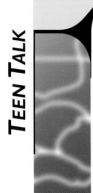

"I always know when I am going to get my period. My favorite pair of jeans doesn't fit me anymore, and my forehead breaks out in pimples. It's annoying, but I can live with it for a few days."—Tamiko, age 14

"My mom teases me that she knows when I have my period. I scream at the dumbest things. My boyfriend, Barry, does guy things with his friends on my PMS days. He says he never knows when I am going to bite his head off."—Kayla, age 15

"I miss school because my head and back hurt so much. I have to concentrate more to finish my homework. I cry a lot, too. I feel so awful that I can't wait for my period to start. Then I know I'll be back to normal soon."—Meagan, age 17

Progesterone is another hormone. It helps the body make a soft lining in the uterus for the egg. The lining is made of blood vessels, tissue, and fluids. It is there to help a baby grow if a sperm fertilizes the egg in the fallopian tube. Sperm are male sex cells that usually are released during sexual intercourse.

Most of the time the egg is not fertilized. It does not stay in the uterus and does not develop into a baby. In this case, the egg breaks down and dissolves. The uterus lining breaks down as well. The egg and lining usually pass from the uterus and through the vagina. The vagina is a canal that leads from the uterus to an outside opening of a female sex organ. This process lasts for three to seven days each month and is known as menstruation. People call menstruation many different names. Some of them are silly. You probably have heard or used some of the names for menstruation: period, friend, curse, monthlies, falling off the roof, and on the rag.

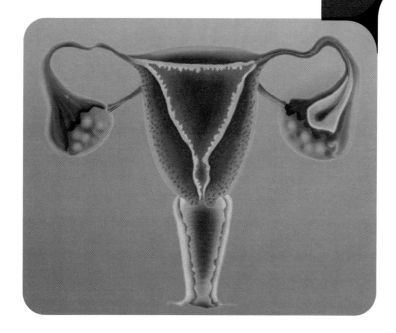

The time from one menstruation to the next is called the menstrual cycle. The menstrual cycle usually lasts 28 days. Some girls and women may have a cycle that is longer or shorter. That is normal, too.

Points to Consider

Do you have PMS symptoms or do you know someone who has PMS symptoms? What are some of the symptoms? How do your symptoms or the symptoms of that person affect you?

What are some of the jokes and teasing you have heard about PMS?

Why do you think some people still do not take PMS seriously?

Chapter Overview

PMS may be an imbalance in hormones and brain chemicals.

PMS is different for each person who has it.

Symptoms of PMS can be mild, moderate, or severe. Severe cases of PMS are rare.

Pain during a period is common, especially in teens, but it is not PMS.

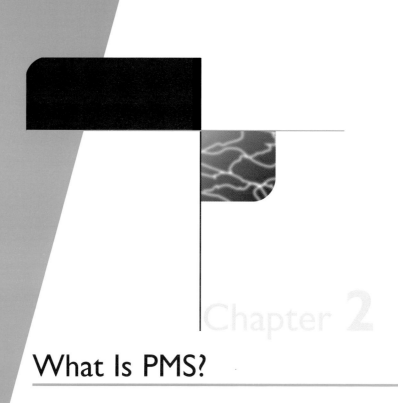

Chapter 2

What Is PMS?

What Causes PMS?

Doctors do not know exactly what causes PMS, so it is hard to define. Most doctors agree that sex hormones and PMS are closely linked. Many doctors think PMS is a reaction to normal hormone levels. No one knows why some girls or women react, or get PMS symptoms, while others do not react.

Many people with severe PMS are treated successfully with low doses of antidepressant drugs. These drugs affect a chemical in the brain called serotonin. Therefore, serotonin may be one neurotransmitter, or brain chemical, involved in PMS. Endorphins are another chemical released by the brain that may be linked to PMS. Today, doctors think PMS probably is unbalanced chemical levels involving both the body's sex hormones and brain neurotransmitters.

Darlene is sitting on the kitchen floor and crying. Her little brother **DARLENE, AGE 14** Billy is running in circles chanting, "U-G-L-Y, you don't have an alibi." Normally, Darlene would tackle Billy playfully and tickle him until he stopped teasing her. Today, she feels too tired and the teasing is making her cry. Her head is throbbing. Darlene just wants to stuff a sock in Billy's mouth to make him shut up.

Who Gets PMS?

PMS occurs most commonly in women who are in their late 20s to 40s. Teens can have PMS, too. Some experts believe that more teens have PMS than we know. These experts think teens may be embarrassed to talk with their doctor about menstrual problems.

FAST FACT

PMS can affect a number of areas that help people perform well in sports. PMS can decrease coordination, reaction time, and dexterity, or ease in movement.

Most doctors agree that PMS can affect any woman who menstruates. Being rich or poor, short or tall, large or small does not matter. PMS symptoms may change as a woman grows older. Some women do not get PMS until they near menopause. Menopause usually happens when a woman is in her late 40s or early 50s. It occurs one year after the last menstrual period.

What Does PMS Feel Like?

PMS is different in everyone. For most women, PMS is fairly mild and may be a little worse only during some months. Some girls and women get both physical and mental symptoms of PMS each month. Some may get only physical PMS symptoms. Others may experience only mood changes.

Awful, bad, crappy, crummy, hideous, skanky, and *yucky* are words teens sometimes use to describe PMS symptoms. These symptoms generally fall into three categories: mild, moderate, and severe. Even women who have mild symptoms have days when they feel terrible, both physically and mentally. Most people who have mild to moderate PMS just wait for their symptoms to go away. They may take pain relievers and try to manage the stress in their life. Chapter 4 talks more about managing PMS.

During PMS, concentrating may be difficult and moods may change suddenly. Feeling a lack of control over emotions may be stressful. This can result in feelings of helplessness, tension, and anxiety.

Physically, the body may retain fluid. This causes clothes to become tighter, joints to swell and ache, and breasts to become tender. People with PMS may suddenly find themselves craving chocolate or salty foods. Even people who normally are healthy eaters may crave and eat potato chips or candy bars.

Yakim's mom has PMS. He always feels like he is walking on

YAKIM, AGE 16

eggshells before his mom gets her period. She yells at him if he gets up late in the morning. She gets angry if he raises his eyebrows at her. Yakim tries to schedule extra hours at work after school during his mom's bad week. Yakim would rather flip burgers than deal with a mom who is flipping out.

PMS can aggravate, or irritate, some conditions. A person may already have acne, allergies, asthma, an infection, or migraine headaches. PMS can cause flare-ups and make these conditions worse than normal.

People with PMS often find that their family and friends treat them differently while they have symptoms. Friends may tell them that they are grumpy and oversensitive. Family members might complain that their loved one with PMS doesn't help around the house or laugh as much.

Severe PMS is serious. It can make a person feel quite sick. She might miss a lot of school, sports practice, or work because she feels so tired and achy. Fighting with friends and family may become a problem if moods swing out of control.

Some women can experience major depression and thoughts of suicide, or killing oneself. Symptoms this severe are not PMS but premenstrual dysphoric disorder (PMDD). PMDD also can make a person so angry that she damages property or physically harms someone. Symptoms this severe, however, are rare.

When It's Not PMS

PMS symptoms can be a lot like the symptoms of other medical problems. PMS is called premenstrual syndrome because it happens before a person gets her period. *Pre* means before. If symptoms are PMS, they stop when a period begins or shortly after that. If PMS symptoms show up at other times of the month, then something else is causing the symptoms. Doctors like to rule out other problems such as diabetes, thyroid disorders, allergies, and depression before diagnosing PMS. Chapter 5 discusses how doctors diagnose PMS.

FAST FACT

Menstrual pain is the number one reason young women miss school.

Cramps

Often, teen girls get painful cramps during their periods. Many people think this is part of PMS, but it is not. The medical term for menstrual pain is *dysmenorrhea*. At least 50 percent of teen girls have dysmenorrhea. The pain usually is in the pelvic area, the abdomen, and the lower back. The pelvic area is the area between the hipbones. The abdomen is the area below the stomach. The pain also can shoot down the legs.

Dysmenorrhea cramps are similar to the pain a woman has when she delivers a baby. In many teen girls, the uterus contracts to push out menstrual blood. This causes some of the pain and discomfort of dysmenorrhea.

The menstrual bleeding itself causes pain, too. When the uterine lining breaks down, it releases a chemical called prostaglandin. Prostaglandin causes blood vessels to narrow so there won't be as much bleeding. This means the uterus gets less oxygen. It is thought that too little oxygen and blood to the uterine muscle causes menstrual pain. Prostaglandin also causes the diarrhea associated with menstruation.

Other conditions may cause menstrual pain, but these other causes are rare in teens. Tumors, fallopian tube infections, and endometriosis all can cause menstrual pain. Endometriosis happens when the lining in the uterus attaches to other parts of the body.

Women and girls who have cramps should talk with their doctor. Usually, this pain can be treated with over-the-counter pain medicines such as ibuprofen. A stronger medicine may be needed if the pain interferes with school, sports, work, or regular activities.

Points to Consider

Why do you think PMS affects everyone differently?

Do you think PMS is easy to cope with? Why or why not?

How do you think PMS affects a girl's or woman's relationships with family and friends?

If someone is having PMS, how do you think other people should treat that person?

Chapter Overview

Doing a PMS profile can help a person figure out which symptoms are most bothersome.

Keeping a PMS journal or calendar can help a person feel more in control of PMS symptoms.

PMS profiles, calendars, and journals help people with PMS and their doctor decide what course of action to take.

Tracking PMS

Chapter 3

Karen took out a notebook and pen from the top drawer of her

KAREN, AGE 15

bedroom dresser. She sat on her bed and opened the notebook. Karen jotted down the day's date and wrote a few words about how she was feeling: "One minute I am happy, the next I feel like Paula and Suki are plotting against me. They're going to the movies this weekend. They didn't even ask me if I wanted to come along! Grumpy, tired, had a headache all day."

A person can take two important steps on her own before talking with a doctor about PMS. The first step is to create a PMS profile. This is easy to do. A sample profile appears on pages 22–23.

Your PMS Profile

Rate each of the symptoms below according to how much you experience them in the days before your period. You can use the following scale.

0 = No symptoms. This doesn't bother me.
1 = Mild. This bothers me a little.
2 = Moderate. Sometimes this symptom interferes with my daily activities.
3 = Severe. This symptom seriously affects my life.

____ 1. Aches and pains

____ 2. Anger

____ 3. Anxiety

____ 4. Binge eating (overeating)

____ 5. Bloating

____ 6. Blurred vision

____ 7. Breast tenderness

____ 8. Clumsiness

____ 9. Confusion

____ 10. Constipation

____ 11. Craving salt

____ 12. Craving sweets

____ 13. Crying spells

____ 14. Demanding

____ 15. Depression

____ 16. Diarrhea

____ 17. Disturbed sleep

____ 18. Energy bursts

____ 19. Fatigue

____ 20. Forgetfulness

____ 21. Grumpiness

____ 22. Headaches

___23. Helplessness

___24. Increased appetite

___25. Increased thirst

___26. Irritability

___27. Lack of concentration

___28. Loneliness

___29. Low self-esteem

___30. Lower backache

___31. Missed school

___32. Missed social activities

___33. Mood swings

___34. Nausea

___35. Overly sensitive

___36. Overreaction

___37. Pimples

___38. Restlessness

___39. Stubbornness

___40. Suicidal thoughts

___41. Suspiciousness

___42. Tension

___43. Vivid dreams

___44. Weight gain

Become a Profiler

The PMS profile is really just a list of the most common PMS symptoms. Space should be left somewhere on the list for adding other possible PMS symptoms. On the line just to the left of each symptom, a person rates how bothersome a symptom is. The rating scale is at the top of the profile. For example, a person who doesn't feel bloated before her period would put a 0 next to that symptom. A person may be so angry before her period that it upsets her family. This person might put a 3 next to that symptom.

Filling out the profile takes awhile. However, the chart makes it easy to tell which symptoms bother a person the most. Filling out the profile helps people with PMS understand that their symptoms are real. A profile shows that symptoms are not just in a person's head. Doing a PMS profile also helps people feel they are getting a handle on their symptoms.

Charting PMS symptoms on a calendar can help a
person feel more in control of PMS. She may feel less
overwhelmed by its symptoms.

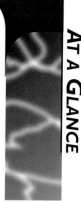

AT A GLANCE

Keeping Track of Symptoms

The next thing to do is to keep a PMS journal or calendar. A
journal can be as simple as a spiral notebook. A calendar looks
like any calendar, but a person tracks her PMS symptoms on it. A
sample calendar is on pages 26–27.

Keeping a journal is like writing short notes to oneself or keeping
a diary. A journal allows more room to add information about
feelings than a calendar does. A calendar, however, may be easier
to read and still has some room for notes about symptoms. Either
tracking system works. A person just needs to choose the method
she is most comfortable with. The important thing is to make time
to do the journal or calendar.

PMS Calendar

Month: October

Monday	Tuesday	Wednesday	
		1	
		feel okay ⟶	
6	7	8	
feel okay ——————————————————————⟶			
13	14	15	
		L slight headache/ cramps	
feel depressed	cramps		
20	21	22	
L	it's over!	feel fine ⟶	
27	28	29	
feel fine ——————————————————————⟶			

Flow Key: L = light, M = medium, H = heavy

	Thursday	Friday	Saturday / Sunday
	2	3	4
			5

→

	9	10	11
		can't concentrate/ crave chocolate	breasts tender
crying			12
			feel depressed

	16	17	18
	M	M	H
			19
	symptoms gone	no symptoms →	M

	23	24	25
			26

→

	30	31	

→

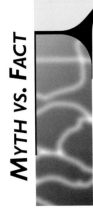
Myth: A woman or girl can get PMS symptoms any time during the month.

Fact: PMS only happens about a few days to two weeks before a period starts. Symptoms can last from a few hours to two weeks. PMS is sometimes followed by a painful period. Once menstruation begins, PMS symptoms should lessen and go away. PMS symptoms that show up other times of the month probably are symptoms of another illness.

A woman or girl should track her symptoms for at least three months. She should write down when symptoms start and stop and the date menstruation begins and ends. It is important to include which symptoms she gets and what days she gets them. Doing all of this can determine her PMS pattern. This information will show when she usually starts getting symptoms. The journal or calendar also should show that the symptoms lessen and stop as menstruation starts. A journal or calendar that shows symptoms all month may indicate a person has a condition other than PMS.

Just doing profiles and calendars or journals makes many girls and women feel better. Taking the time to do these two things helps a person organize thoughts and concentrate on managing her PMS. Writing down symptoms every day may help the person with PMS feel less overwhelmed.

The Next Step

Girls and women can better decide their next step after tracking and profiling symptoms for three months. Most PMS symptoms can be lessened if a person with PMS makes some lifestyle changes. These are changes in the way she lives. The next chapter suggests lifestyle changes that can help manage PMS.

A person should share her PMS information with her doctor at her next regular appointment. Either a family doctor or a gynecologist can help. A gynecologist is a doctor who specializes in the female reproductive system. A family doctor usually can recommend a gynecologist for women who do not have one. Chapters 5 and 6 discuss how doctors diagnose and treat PMS.

A person with severe PMS symptoms should make an appointment with a doctor. A symptom is severe if it keeps a person from school, work, sports, or regular activities. A girl should talk with her family about health coverage before contacting a doctor. People who do not have a doctor can look in the telephone book under *Physicians* or *Clinics* for help. A school nurse or counselor may be able to make a recommendation, too.

Points to Consider

Do you think keeping a PMS journal or a PMS calendar to track symptoms would be worthwhile? Why or why not?

In what ways are PMS profiles, journals, and calendars helpful?

What are the most important things to tell a doctor if a person thinks she has PMS?

Chapter
Overview

Most women and girls can make their PMS symptoms better by doing things on their own.

Healthy eating and regular exercise are the two biggest lifestyle changes that can improve PMS.

Reducing stress helps the body fight PMS.

Plenty of water and rest help reduce the symptoms of PMS.

Chapter 4

Making Healthy Changes

Tala's doctor gave her a list of foods that she should avoid to reduce PMS symptoms. "I can't do this!" said Tala when she saw all of the foods on the list. Dr. Sylvester told her that staying away from just some of the foods could make a difference. The doctor asked Tala if she thought she could avoid three or four foods to start. Then Tala could avoid a few more foods later. Tala said she would try it for a few months. Anything was better than how she felt when she had PMS.

TALA, AGE 14

Self-Help

Many people with PMS can reduce their symptoms through self-help, or doing things on their own. A doctor, teacher, or other trusted adult may be able to give someone with PMS advice and help. Self-help ideas are lifestyle changes. That means a person changes the way she lives to beat PMS. It might be thought of this way. Dealing with PMS can feel like walking a tightrope. A person would not wear clunky shoes and carry a wriggling puppy while crossing a tightrope. Instead, a person would do her best to stay balanced and cross the tightrope without falling.

A person can take some action on her own to help her stay balanced while walking the PMS tightrope. Exercising regularly and paying attention to diet are the two main ways to fight PMS symptoms. Reducing stress, drinking lots of water, and getting plenty of rest help, too.

Premenstrual Syndrome

It's better to eat six smaller meals than three bigger ones during PMS. Not going longer than 2½ to 3 hours without eating helps keep the sugar level in the blood even. Bouncing blood-sugar levels can cause headaches that often are made worse by PMS.

Eating right, exercising, and learning to relax can help a person with PMS stay balanced. Eating the wrong foods, sitting around, and feeling tense are like the clunky shoes and wriggling puppy. A person might be able to cross the tightrope and get through PMS under these circumstances. However, it will be at the expense of being more tired, sore, and miserable.

Food Fighters

How and what a person eats could be one of the best weapons against PMS. Changing eating habits can help people feel better and lessen PMS symptoms. Some doctors think that diet is important because certain foods can affect serotonin. The amount of serotonin females have probably is linked to emotional PMS symptoms such as moodiness, anxiety, and depression. A healthy diet also helps keep the mind and body strong. Avoiding certain foods can help relieve some symptoms.

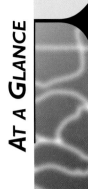

Foods to avoid just before and during PMS are:

Sugar, honey, molasses, and artificial sweeteners

Caffeine, including chocolate, coffee, tea, cola, diet cola, and even decaffeinated drinks

Foods made with white flour such as doughnuts, white bread, and some pasta

Sweet juices such as cherry and prune

Here are some tips for diet changes that can help to fight PMS as well as cramps:

Decrease salt. Salt can cause fluid retention, bloating, and breast soreness. Stay away from salty foods such as potato chips, hot dogs, and frozen or microwave dinners. Watch out for hidden salt. A fast-food shake contains enough salt to make PMS worse. Ask someone or read a food label to find out how much salt, or sodium, is in a food.

Avoid foods and drinks with caffeine. Coffee, cola, tea, and chocolate are some items to avoid. Even decaffeinated drinks have some caffeine. Caffeine can cause moodiness, tension, and breast tenderness.

Eat more grains, potatoes, beans, and rice. These foods are called complex carbohydrates. Some complex carbohydrates help build serotonin levels in the body.

Eat fewer sugary foods and sugars. Cut back on sugar, artificial sweeteners, colas, candy, honey, and molasses. Sweets can make a person feel tired and tense after the first burst of energy.

Eat low-fat foods. Try especially to eat low-fat dairy foods. Soy milk is a good option. The body uses fat in foods made from milk, such as cheese, butter, and ice cream, to make prostaglandin. Prostaglandin is a chemical that may cause cramps.

Eat vegetables. Most vegetables have nutrients in them such as magnesium and calcium that can help lessen PMS symptoms. Many vegetables are full of fiber. This substance can help reduce abdominal bloating.

Overall, it is important to stay a healthy weight so the body works its best. Many doctors recommend that women and girls eat small meals more often than three times a day during menstruation. For example, a person might eat six smaller meals instead of eating just breakfast, lunch, and dinner. She should at least eat light snacks in between three main meals. Eating more often helps keep the blood-sugar level even. These levels are related to headaches.

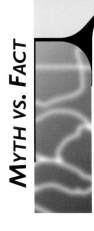

Myth: A person shouldn't exercise when having PMS because PMS affects coordination and makes a person tired.

Fact: Exercising at least three to five times a week helps. It can make a person feel better and less tense, especially during menstruation.

Exercise

Some studies show that regular exercise can reduce some PMS symptoms. People who exercise at least three times a week have milder PMS symptoms than those who don't exercise. Aerobic exercise is best. This is the kind of exercise that gets the heart and blood pumping. Some examples of aerobic exercise include running, jogging, walking fast, swimming, and biking. Most doctors recommend exercising 20 to 30 minutes 3 to 5 times a week.

Exercise produces hormones in the body called endorphins. Maybe you have heard of runners feeling happy after exercise. Some people call this a "runner's high." Endorphins move through the body during exercise and help make a person feel better. Endorphins naturally relieve stress, tension, and depression. So, it makes sense that regular exercise could lessen these PMS symptoms.

Stress Reduction

Reducing stress also helps lessen PMS. That is easier said than done. Still, learning to relax is important. People cannot change all of the things in their life that make them tense. People may not have much control over home life and school. However, people can change how they react to the things that cause them stress.

The things that cause stress are called stress triggers. It is a good idea to avoid stress triggers if possible. A person cannot get away from all triggers. People can learn some tricks to help them relax and feel less tense when a trigger pops. It may be necessary to experiment and find what works best. Here are some options to try:

Breathe deeply, count to 10 (or 20 or 30 if necessary), and exhale, or breathe out, slowly.

Take a long, hot bath.

Close your eyes and think about one of your favorite places. Imagine that you are there. Breathe deeply and slowly. Listen to your breathing and try to shut out other noises.

Listen to soothing music.

Walk around the block.

Take a nap.

Call, write, or e-mail a friend.

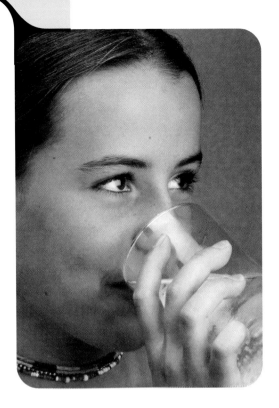

Water

Drinking as much water as possible can help people with PMS. Many people stop drinking water when they have PMS because their body retains fluid and they feel bloated. However, if a person doesn't drink a lot of water, the body starts to hold in fluid. That causes even more bloating. Drinking a lot of water actually helps the body rid itself of more fluids.

Rest

Finally, a person should get plenty of rest when she has PMS symptoms. Actually, plenty of sleep is a good idea all of the time. It is especially important during PMS, though. Not enough sleep can make a person tired, tense, and moody. PMS makes these feelings even worse. Sneaking in a nap can help.

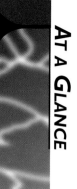

AT A GLANCE

Five ways to reduce PMS symptoms:

1. Eat healthier foods.

2. Exercise three to five times a week.

3. Eat less salt or eat fewer salty foods.

4. Stay away from caffeine.

5. Relax.

Points to Consider

Give an example of the meals a person should eat for one day during PMS.

What kind of exercise could a person do to help reduce PMS? How can a person fit this activity into a busy schedule?

What are three things you do that help you to feel more relaxed?

What would be an easy reminder to drink plenty of water each day?

Chapter Overview

Up to 20 percent of people still experience serious PMS symptoms. This is even after eating healthier diets, exercising, and reducing stress.

There are no medical tests that can determine if a person has PMS.

A doctor may do a pelvic exam to rule out other possible causes of some PMS symptoms.

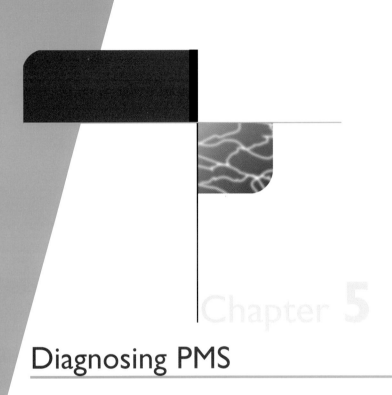

Chapter **5**

Diagnosing PMS

Some people still experience serious PMS symptoms even after eating right, exercising more, and managing stress. The good news is that only around 20 percent of people with PMS need more help. PMS symptoms cause these girls and women to miss school, work, and regular activities. These people also may have problems sleeping. They may have difficulty getting along with family, friends, and coworkers when they have PMS.

Usually, medication is tried last for people with PMS. Because the cause of PMS is unknown, there is no single medicine or treatment for PMS. A doctor focuses on treating a person's symptoms. For example, if a person has depression that keeps her in bed, the doctor might prescribe an antidepressant medicine. Each person is different. A doctor works with each woman or girl individually to see which treatments work best for her.

At the Doctor's Office

Ardath made an appointment with her family doctor. When *ARDATH, AGE 16* she was in the doctor's office, she showed the doctor her PMS profile and calendar. The doctor said it looked like Ardath had PMS. However, Dr. Vang wanted to do some tests to make sure Ardath did not have any other illnesses. The nurse took some blood from Ardath's arm. The doctor talked with Ardath about her worst PMS symptom, her headaches. They looked at Ardath's calendar and saw that her headaches usually started a week before her period. The doctor recommended that Ardath start taking ibuprofen just before her symptoms usually started. Ardath made another appointment before she left the office to go over the results of her tests.

DID YOU KNOW?

English doctor Katharina Dalton is considered a pioneer in PMS. She worked for years to get the medical community to recognize PMS.

Diagnosing PMS can be difficult. There are no lab or blood tests to use that can figure out if symptoms are PMS. A doctor might take a blood test to check for other illnesses. A profile and journal or calendar help a doctor tell if symptoms are PMS. Symptoms are likely to be PMS if they happen just before a person's period and return every month.

The doctor may perform a pelvic exam. This exam can help the doctor determine that physical causes are not responsible for any PMS symptoms. These physical causes are rare in teens, but the doctor may want to rule them out.

A pelvic exam can be scary and awkward. A pelvic exam may be uncomfortable, but it should not hurt. If the doctor performing the exam is a man, another woman usually is present in the room. If another woman is not present, the patient can ask to have a woman in the room. A pelvic exam usually is much less scary if the person is relaxed. Some people chat with their doctor about school or the weather during the exam. Other people just close their eyes and breathe deeply. It is important for a person to do whatever makes her feel calm.

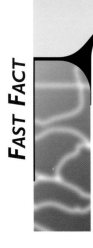

FAST FACT

PMS is a chronic, or long-lasting, condition. However, many people with PMS can manage the condition through self-help and lifestyle changes. Such actions help as many as 80 percent of these women and girls.

A pelvic exam begins with checking the genitals, or outer sex organs. The doctor should touch a person respectfully. He or she is looking for signs of infections. The doctor uses a speculum during the next part of the exam. A speculum is a metal or plastic tool used to open the vagina. This allows the doctor to see the cervix, or the opening to the uterus, and the vagina. This part of the exam can feel uncomfortable, so trying to relax is important.

During the last part of the exam, the doctor inserts his or her fingers into the vagina and rectum. The rectum is the lowest portion of the large intestine. The doctor also places a hand on the belly. The doctor does this to feel the ovaries and uterus. Once again, the doctor is looking for infections or signs of other conditions.

After the exam, the doctor may ask the person to schedule another appointment to complete blood tests. Usually at this point, the doctor talks with the person about PMS. He or she also discusses what can be done to relieve symptoms.

Points to Consider

Some people exercise, avoid stress, and eat a healthy diet yet still have PMS symptoms. How do you think that would feel?

When should a person with PMS schedule a doctor's appointment?

What are some things a person could do to relax during a pelvic exam?

Chapter Overview

Medication may help women and girls who do not see an improvement in their PMS after lifestyle changes.

No one medicine can treat PMS. A doctor may recommend one or more of many medications, or traditional treatments.

Several nontraditional treatments have helped some people with PMS.

Chapter **6**

Treating PMS Symptoms

Traditional Treatments

There are many medications that a doctor might prescribe for PMS symptoms. Medicines are usually thought of as traditional treatments. The best medicine for a person depends not only on her symptoms but also on how her body reacts. A person may have to try a few different medicines or take more than one drug.

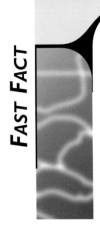
Some of the drugs a doctor might prescribe are:

Hormones, such as birth control pills. These help balance the body's own hormone levels. Hormone therapy has been used for many years to relieve PMS symptoms. Birth control pills or injections relieve symptoms or temporarily stop ovulation and menstruation in severe PMS cases.

Nonsteroidal anti-inflammatory drugs (NSAIDs). These relieve aches, headaches, and breast tenderness. They also relieve cramps. Ibuprofen is a common NSAID. Taking over-the-counter pain relievers can help on especially bad days with painful symptoms. A doctor might prescribe a pain reliever that is stronger than an over-the-counter medicine.

Antidepressants. These may ease emotional symptoms of PMS such as anger, anxiety, and depression. Doctors usually prescribe these drugs at lower doses than when they are used to treat depression. Some doctors may recommend that a person take these drugs only during the two weeks before menstruation.

Diuretics. These can reduce the weight gain and bloating caused by fluid retention.

Nontraditional Treatments

Serena takes a prescription pain reliever for her PMS aches and pains. Her doctor also told her about taking extra vitamin E for her breast soreness. Serena recently read an article about vitamin B and PMS. She plans to talk with her doctor at her next appointment. Serena wants to know more about trying vitamin B for some of her other PMS symptoms.

More often than ever before, people with PMS are asking their doctor about treatments other than drugs. A number of nontraditional treatments have been shown to reduce PMS symptoms for some women. Anyone who wants to try a nontraditional treatment for PMS should talk with her doctor. A doctor is a woman's partner in treating PMS. The doctor should at least be told all methods a person is using to deal with PMS symptoms. Together, the doctor and patient can create a treatment plan. It might include self-help, medication, and nontraditional treatments.

Some nontraditional treatments are:

Vitamin and mineral supplements. Some studies show that vitamin E, vitamin B, and calcium tablets can help ease PMS symptoms. Too much of these supplements in the diet, however, can cause side effects.

Herbs. Some people with PMS have found that herbal treatments, or remedies, help their symptoms. Again, talk with a doctor about the kinds of herbs to try. Dandelion, evening primrose oil, flaxseed oil, St. John's wort, raspberry leaf tea, oatstraw, and cleavers are common herbal treatments.

Heat and massage. Heat on the stomach and lower back can relieve PMS symptoms as well as cramps. A deep muscle massage can help achy joints and muscles. A massage also can ease tension or anxiety.

Sunlight. Some people say that sunlight lifts their mood and helps lessen the emotional symptoms of PMS. Sunlight raises serotonin levels in the brain. During the summer, getting one-half hour of fresh air each day may help. In the winter, some people with PMS sit in front of special lights similar to sunlight. These lights, however, do not tan the skin.

PMS Escape®. This is a powdered, fruit-flavored drink that contains carbohydrates, vitamins, and minerals. Some studies have shown that this product helps relieve PMS-related depression.

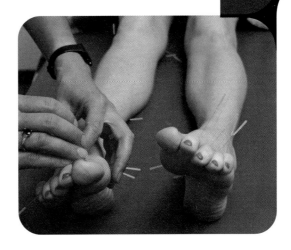

Some other nontraditional treatments are:

Acupuncture: Chinese practice of placing needles on the body to relieve pain or cure illness

Acupressure: a technique that uses the same points on the body used in acupuncture; however, massage is used instead of needles on these points.

Reflexology: massage and pressure with hands on specific points of the body; these body points are believed to benefit other parts of the body.

Meditation: a process of deep and focused thought

Yoga: a system of exercises for achieving well-being

Points to Consider

What kinds of medicines have you or someone you know tried for PMS? How did the medicines work?

What do you think of nontraditional treatment for PMS?

Do you think treating PMS is a challenge? Why or why not?

Chapter Overview

Recognizing that a person has PMS is one of the first steps to controlling it.

People can do even more than making healthy changes and seeing a doctor to keep PMS under control.

Even if you don't have PMS, you probably know someone who does. You can do several things to help that person beat her PMS symptoms.

Chapter 7

Taking Control of PMS

"Get out of my face, you little brat," Chante screamed at her sister. "If you touch my stuff again, I'm going to lock you in the closet." Chante's little sister ran from the room crying. Latifah hated Chante when she was like this. All she wanted to do was try Chante's perfume.

One of the worst things a person can do when she has PMS is ignore the symptoms. She should listen if friends and family tell her that once a month she turns into a different person. Other people may recognize a behavior pattern more easily than the person herself can. The person should take time to do a PMS profile and journal or calendar. The first step in taking control of PMS is recognizing its symptoms and admitting to having them.

The next step is to try the self-help ideas in chapter 4 of this book. A woman or girl should work with her doctor to develop a treatment plan for PMS symptoms. Here are more ways women can control PMS and keep it from controlling them.

Be a sponge. Soak up whatever information you can about PMS. Talk with your doctor, school nurse, teacher, friends, and family about PMS. Read books and magazines. Search the Internet. Ask questions. The more you know, the more in control you will feel. Use the resources listed in the back of this book to get started.

Lighten up. It's okay to admit you have PMS. It's even okay to laugh at PMS jokes. PMS comes in cycles, so try to be patient and considerate when you know your PMS is coming. Laugh as often as possible. It can help you feel and look better.

Plan for PMS. Out-of-control PMS symptoms can damage relationships with friends and family. Ask for help and support. Reduce stress by telling family and friends when your symptoms are about to start. Let them know what you can and cannot do while you have PMS. Plan ahead and do extra things on days when you don't have PMS. Then you can take it easier when PMS strikes.

Take care of you. Figure out what you need to do to beat PMS. Accept help. This can be hard to do. Start by talking with friends and family about what may make life easier for you while you have PMS. Ask for one thing that you need. An example might be quiet time when you get home from school. Don't forget to thank family and friends when they help you out. Find time every day to do one activity you enjoy. This may be as simple as listening to the birds at the bus stop in the morning.

Get more help if you need it. Sometimes everything you, your friends, and your family do still is not enough. PMS symptoms still may make life miserable. Don't give up. See your doctor. Go to a counselor or support group. Check the telephone book listings for *Psychiatrist, Psychologist,* or *Counselor.* All of these medical professionals can help.

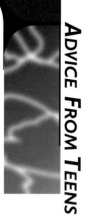

"My friend Cecelia and I have a contest going on. Whenever we see each other, the first person to tell a joke and make the other one laugh wins a point. Rack up 10 points and the loser buys lunch. It's a great way to take a minute and laugh, no matter how you feel."
—Lori, age 15

On the Outside Looking In

You may not have PMS. However, you probably know someone who does. Maybe it is your mom, sister, aunt, grandmother, friend, or girlfriend. You can help make sure the one you care about takes control of her PMS symptoms.

"I used to run and hide when my mom was 'PMS-ing.' Some days she screams louder than squealing tires. Then my girlfriend, Sherise, told me about something she does with her sister. Now, I can do something to help whenever my mom gets worked up and gets in my face. I just keep repeating, 'Mom, I love you. Mom, I love you.' Eventually she stops hollering and breaks into a big grin. Some days I have to say 'Mom, I love you' until my head hurts. It's worth it, though. It keeps me from saying something stupid, and it helps her get back under control."

NATE, AGE 18

"I stopped drinking cola. I also try to take time every morning to breathe deeply and clear my head. I do this just for a few minutes before I jump into the shower for school. I used a PMS calendar for a while. Now I can figure out when my PMS symptoms will start. Right before I think they are going to start, I tape a to-do list on the refrigerator every day. The list says what I am going to get done. It might list certain chores, homework, and baby-sitting Zach and Andrew. That way my mom knows what to expect from me. We don't fight as much now. My headaches hurt less, and my acne outbreaks don't last as long, either."
—Nancy, age 18

Some of the things you can do to help someone with PMS are:

Learn. Find out about PMS from a doctor, teacher, or other trusted adult. Use the resources listed in the back of this book to find out more information.

Listen. Be supportive and reassure her.

Forgive. Don't take angry outbursts personally. A person with PMS sometimes can't control her emotions, no matter how hard she tries. Keep in mind that PMS will pass, eventually. Laugh if you can. If you can't laugh, walk away.

Support. Do activities with your loved one who has PMS. Get outdoors in the fresh air and sun. Exercise together. Fix a healthy snack and share it. Tell her you love her.

Points to Consider

Who would you talk with to learn more about PMS?

What are three things that you like to do just for yourself? How do these activities make you feel?

How could a person plan with her friends and family for PMS?

What are two things you could do for someone who has PMS to make her life less stressful?

Glossary

diagnose (dye-uhg-NOHSS)—to determine what disease someone has or to figure out the cause of an illness

dysmenorrhea (diss-men-or-REE-uh)—menstrual pain

endorphin (en-DOR-fin)—a substance created by the brain that reduces pain

estrogen (ESS-truh-juhn)—a female sex hormone

herb (URB)—a plant with leaves or seeds that is used for medicine or cooking

hormone (HOR-mohn)—a chemical that controls a body function

massage (MUH-sahzh)—to rub someone's body to loosen muscles or to help the person relax

menstruation (men-stroo-AYE-shuhn)—the monthly discharge of blood, fluids, and tissue from the uterus in nonpregnant females

ovulation (ov-yuh-LAY-shuhn)—the release of an egg from the ovary

premenstrual syndrome (PREE-men-stroo-wuhl SIN-drohm)—a group of physical and mental symptoms that may occur in a female before menstruation

progesterone (proh-JESS-tuh-rohn)—a female sex hormone that prepares the lining of the uterus for an egg released from an ovary

prostaglandin (pross-tuh-GLAN-din)—a substance that causes the muscle of the uterus to contract

puberty (PYOO-bur-tee)—the time when a person's body physically changes from a child's to an adult's

speculum (SPE-kyoo-lum)—a metal or plastic tool used by a doctor to gently open a woman's vagina during an exam

symptom (SIMP-tuhm)—evidence of a disease or medical condition

For More Information

Bourgeois, Paulette, and Martin Wolfish. *Changes in You and Me: A Book About Puberty, Mostly for Girls.* Kansas City: Andrews McMeel, 1994.

Dalton, Katharina, and Wendy Holton. *Once a Month: Understanding and Treating PMS.* Alameda, CA: Hunter House, 1999.

Gravelle, Karen, and Jennifer Gravelle. *The Period Book: Everything You Don't Want to Ask (but Need to Know).* New York: Walker and Co., 1996.

Harris, Robie H. *It's Perfectly Normal: A Book About Changing Bodies, Growing Up, Sex, and Sexual Health.* Cambridge, MA: Candlewick Press, 1994.

Useful Addresses and Internet Sites

American College of Obstetricians and
Gynecologists (ACOG)
409 12th Street Southwest
PO Box 96920
Washington, DC 20090-6920
www.acog.org

Canadian Women's Health Network (CWHN)
Suite 203
419 Graham Avenue
Winnipeg MB R3C OM3
CANADA
1-888-818-9172
www.cwhn.ca

National Women's Health Information Center
(NWHIC)
Office on Women's Health
U.S. Department of Health and Human
Services
200 Independence Avenue Southwest
Room 730B
Washington, DC 20201
1-800-994-WOMAN (800-994-9662)
www.4woman.gov

Women's Health Bureau
Health Canada
0911A Brooke Claxton Building
Tunney's Pasture
Ottawa ON K1A OK9
CANADA
www.hc-sc.gc.ca/pcb/whb

Always a woman: Always growing
www.alwaysawoman.com/growing/index.html
Provides downloadable calendar, teen message
board, and information on doctors and talking
with mom in relation to PMS

Body talk for teens
www.bayercare.com/midol/teens/talkteen.html
Gives information about puberty and
menstruation

KidsHealth.org for teens
www.kidshealth.org/teen/bodymind/
menstruation.html
Gives girls and guys information on
menstruation

Kotex GirlSpace: That Time of the Month
www.kotex.com/girlspace/time
Contains a printable period calendar as well as
information on PMS, exercise, and nutrition

Mayo Clinic Health Oasis
www.mayohealth.org/mayo/pted/htm/
pms_sb.htm
Provides dietary suggestions for PMS
symptoms

U.S. Food and Drug Administration
www.fda.gov/opacom/catalog/ots_mens.html
Contains article for teens about the menstrual
cycle

Index

aches, 16, 17, 22, 48, 50

acne, 8, 10, 17

acupressure, 51

acupuncture, 51

anger, 6, 7, 8, 17, 48. *See also* mood swings

antidepressants, 14, 42, 48

anxiety, 7, 33, 48, 50

birth control pills, 48

bloating, 7, 8, 34, 35, 38, 48

blood tests, 43, 44

blood-sugar levels, 33, 35

brain chemicals, 14. *See also* endorphins; serotonin

breast tenderness, 7, 16, 34, 48

caffeine, 34

calcium, 35, 48

calendar (PMS), 20, 25–28, 43, 54

carbohydrates, complex, 34

cervix, 44

concentration, lack of, 8, 10, 16

control, lack of, 16, 36

controlling PMS, 53–59

cramps, 18–19, 34, 48, 50

Dalton, Katharina, 43

depression, 17, 33, 36, 42, 48, 50. *See also* mood swings

diagnosing PMS, 41–45

diarrhea, 8, 18, 22

diet, 30, 32–33, 34–35

diuretics, 48

doctors, 29, 42–44, 49

drugs. *See* medication

dysmenorrhea, 18. *See also* cramps

eating. *See* diet

eggs, 9–10

emotions, 16–17. *See also* mood swings

endometriosis, 19

endometrium, 9

endorphins, 14, 36

estrogen, 9

exercise, 30, 32–33, 36

fallopian tubes, 9
     infection in, 19

family and friends, 6, 9, 16, 17, 54, 55

fiber, 35

fluid retention, 16, 34, 38, 48

food cravings, 8, 16

foods to avoid, 34. *See also* diet

glossary, 60

gynecologists, 29. *See also* doctors

headaches, 7, 33, 35, 48

heat, 50

herbs, 50

hormones, 9–10, 13, 48

ibuprofen, 19, 48

journal (PMS), 20, 25–28, 43, 54

laughter, 55, 57

low-fat foods, 35

magnesium, 35

massage, 50

medication, 42, 46, 47–48. *See also* antidepressants; ibuprofen

Index continued

meditation, 51
menopause, 15
menstrual cycle, 11
menstruation
    average age of beginning, 9
    definition of, 10
mineral supplements, 50
mood swings, 7, 16, 17, 33, 34, 38. *See also* anger

nonsteroidal anti-inflammatory drugs (NSAIDs), 48

ovaries, 9, 44
ovulation, 9

pelvic exam, 43–44
period. *See* menstruation
planning for PMS, 55
PMS Escape®, 50
premenstrual dysphoric disorder (PMDD), 17
premenstrual syndrome (PMS)
    causes of, 13–14
    controlling, 53–59
    diagnosing, 41–45
    how it feels, 15–17
    planning for, 55
    who gets it, 14–15
profile (PMS), 20–24, 28, 43, 54
progesterone, 10
prostaglandin, 18, 35
puberty, 9

rectum, 44
reflexology, 51
rest, 30, 32, 38

salt, 34
self-help, 32–38
serotonin, 14, 33, 34, 50
speculum, 44
sperm, 10
stress, 30, 32–33, 36–37
sugar, 35
sunlight, 50
symptoms, 7–8, 15–17, 28, 40, 50
    and eating habits, 33–35
    physical changes, 8
    profiling, 21–24, 28
    psychological changes, 8
    self-help for, 30, 32–38
    treating, 42, 47–51

tension, 34, 36, 38, 50
tiredness, 38
treatments
    nontraditional, 49–51
    traditional, 47–48
tumors, 19

uterus, 9–10, 18, 44

vagina, 10, 44
vegetables, 35
vitamins, 49, 50

water, 30, 32, 38
weight
    gain caused by fluid retention, 16, 48
    maintaining a healthy, 35

yoga, 51